Truffle's Christmas

To McGregor, Bramble, Acorn and all their companions and successors,
with my love,
A.C.

First published in the United Kingdom in 2000
by David Bennett Books Limited.

Text copyright © 2000 Anna Currey.
Illustrations copyright © 2000 Anna Currey.
Truffle character copyright © 2000 Anna Currey.

Anna Currey asserts her moral right to be identified
as the author and illustrator of this work.

BRITISH LIBRARY CATALOGUING-IN-PUBLICATION DATA
A catalogue record of this book is available from the British Library.

Printed in China

ISBN 1 85602 378 8

Truffle's Christmas

Written & Illustrated by
Anna Currey

DAVID BENNETT BOOKS

Christmas was coming.

All the little mice had finished their letters to Santa.

All, that is, except for Truffle.
He couldn't decide
what he wanted.

"I'd really love a hula hoop…

but I wish we had a blanket, a nice new blanket without any holes…

but, there again…"

"You'll have to decide,"
said Emmeline,
his big sister, who
always knew best,
"or Santa won't
bring you anything.
Here, you'd better
start again."

"Oh all right, a hula
hoop then," said Truffle,
throwing away his letter.

He put his new letter into an
envelope and addressed it to
'SANTER KLORS, NORF POL'.

On Christmas Eve the mice hung their stockings
up in a neat row.

"I'm getting a nurse's uniform," announced Emmeline.
"I'm getting a chemistry set," said George,
Truffle's big brother.
The littlest mice squeaked excitedly; they wanted
teddy bears. Then all the mice went off to bed.

Mother Mouse
put their blanket
over them and
tucked them in.

It wasn't a very big blanket and didn't
quite cover them all.

Emmeline got most of the blanket because she was the
oldest, then George, then Truffle. But the littlest mice were
right on the edge. They lay shivering in the cold.

So Truffle gave them his part of the blanket,
but then he got cold.

"Bother," said Truffle, as he stared out into the darkness.
"I wish I'd asked for a blanket and not a hula hoop.
Bother... I know," he said, suddenly sitting bolt upright.
"I'll wait for Santa
to tell him
I've changed
my mind."

Truffle crept out of bed and tiptoed
to the mousehole door.

There he waited and waited,
but Santa didn't come, and didn't come.
"It's no use here," grumbled Truffle,
"I'll go outside where I can see farther."

"I'd better take
something
to eat in case
I get hungry."

He packed an apple
core, a bread crust
and half a peanut,
and he went off into
the night, dragging
his picnic behind him.

It was very cold.

As he waited for Santa,
Truffle became hungry,
so he unpacked his
picnic. First he ate his
bread crust, very slowly.

Then he ate his apple
core, very, *very* slowly.

Finally he ate his peanut half, *very, very* slowly.

But still Santa
did not come.
Truffle stood up
and brushed
his whiskers.

"I will go to that hill over there, where I can
see Santa and Santa can see me," he said firmly,
and plodded off.

In the woods a fox barked and an owl hooted.
A tabby cat pricked up her ears. Truffle was
scared, but he trudged on and on.

The clouds covered the
moon. The candle in
Truffle's lantern went out.
It was very dark.

Truffle felt all alone, and very tired. He sat down and tried to watch for Santa but his eyes kept shutting. Softly, it started to snow. Truffle fell asleep.

"Now!" said the fox,
"before the snow covers him entirely."

"Now!" said the owl,
"before the greedy fox gets him."

"Now!" said the tabby cat,
"because I'm very, very hungry."

Then, just before the fox jumped and the owl swooped and the tabby cat pounced...

… there was a tinkling
and jingling of sleigh bells.

There was a rattling
and creaking of harnesses.

There was a pattering
and shuffling of hooves.
But Truffle was fast asleep
and didn't notice a thing…

... until a reindeer
snorted in his face.

"Eek!" squeaked Truffle.

"What's this?" said Santa. "A mouse! A poor little mouse. How cold you are."

Truffle shivered.

"Why aren't you tucked up in bed?" asked Santa.
"I came out to find you," mumbled Truffle, still half asleep and rather muddled.
"I wanted a hula hoop… but we really need a blanket."
"Hmm," said Santa, "I think it's time I took you home."
He tucked Truffle into his pocket…

... and away they went.
Over the fox, the owl
and the tabby cat.
Over the forest and hills.
Over the fields and hedges.

And they didn't touch the ground until
they reached Truffle's home.

Truffle was asleep again. So fast asleep that he didn't even stir when Santa fished him out of his pocket and returned him to the mousehole.

Santa's hand brushed against a little piece of crumpled paper, lying on the ground.

He unfolded it carefully.

'Deer Santer,' it said in tiny mouse letters,
'I wood lik a hoola hup, blankit, hulla hoop, blankit.'

"Aha!" said Santa.
"I see!"

Emmeline was the first to wake up on Christmas morning. She squealed loudly and woke up George, Truffle, and the littlest mice.

They all squealed, too. For not only were they lying under the reddest, warmest, cosiest blanket that had ever been, they were lying on the most beautiful bed (for mice) in the world.

And Emmeline had her nurse's uniform...

George had his chemistry set...

the littlest mice had their tiny teddy bears...

... and Truffle had his hula hoop!

He smiled happily, and on his whiskers
there still clung a little bit of red fluff
from the bottom of Santa's pocket.